WHAT HAPPENS NEXT?
JANINA DOMANSKA

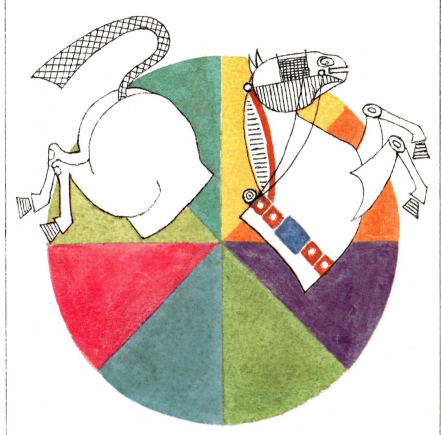

GREENWILLOW BOOKS
NEW YORK

Copyright © 1983 by Janina Domanska. All rights reserved. No part of this book may be reproduced or utilized in any form or by any means, electronic or mechanical, including photocopying, recording or by any information storage and retrieval system, without permission in writing from the Publisher, Greenwillow Books, a division of William Morrow & Company, Inc., 105 Madison Avenue, New York, N.Y. 10016. Printed in the United States of America. First Edition 10 9 8 7 6 5 4 3 2 1

Library of Congress Cataloging in Publication Data
Domanska, Janina. What happens next?
Summary: A baron who loves tall tales promises to free the peasant who can tell him a tale that will surprise him.
[1. Storytelling—Fiction. 2. Middle Ages—Fiction] I. Title.
PZ7.D710Wh 1983 [E] 82-24219
ISBN 0-688-01748-7 ISBN 0-688-01749-5 (lib. bdg.)

TO ERNEST NOSSEN WITH LOVE

Once there lived a baron who loved tall tales and never tired of listening to them. But there came a time in his life when he thought he had heard them all. And so one day he called his peasants together and said, "If any one of you can tell me a tale that will surprise me, I will give him his freedom."

The peasants stood silent and hesitating until finally a young peasant stepped forward. The baron nodded to him and the young man began.

"Yesterday, as I drove to the field, my horse seemed to stumble, then he shook himself, and before my eyes he split himself in two. His front half hurried home and his back half followed neighing."

"Who would believe that?" the courtiers said.
"Don't interrupt. Let him continue his story," the baron said.
"Once home, the two halves joined together and the horse stood whole again. I tied him to the old willow tree, and lay down beneath it to rest.

"I fell asleep, and when I awoke, the willow had grown so high that its tip touched the sky. How nice, I thought to myself, and climbed up."

"Sheer nonsense!" cried the courtiers.

"Very interesting," said the baron, and asked the young man to continue.

"I strolled around and looked about for a while, but when I returned to the willow to climb down, it withered away.

"I didn't know what to do until, below me, on earth, I saw a peasant separating wheat from chaff. The chaff flew up to the sky and I gathered as much as I could and twisted it into a rope."

"You can't make a rope out of chaff," protested the courtiers.

But the baron smiled and said, "Go on. What happened next?"

"When my rope was finished, I attached one end of it to the sky, and started down. But halfway down I was stopped in midair. The rope was too short. So I unfastened the top and added it to the bottom."

The courtiers had had enough.

"Ridiculous," they cried.

"No," said the baron, "our storyteller is quite clever," and he motioned the peasant to go on.

"I continued climbing down, but when I was about fifty feet from the ground, the rope stopped short again.

"I jumped down and landed in a swamp.

"Though I stayed where I was, I hurried home for a shovel to dig myself out."

"Rubbish! Rubbish!" shouted the courtiers.
But the baron urged the peasant to continue.
"Once out of the swamp, I jumped into the river to wash myself.

"I dried in the water and went on my way.

"In a meadow, an old herdsman was tending the flocks. 'Good morning, dear herdsman!' I said. 'I am not a herdsman,' the man replied angrily. 'I am the baron's father!'"

The baron cried out, "Impossible! My father tending sheep! That would surprise me!"

"In that case," the peasant said quickly, "it is time to set me free as you promised."

And the baron did.